The Long Dive

by Mr and Mrs Smith

A JONATHAN CAPE BOOK

Atheneum   1979   New York

For Henry

Copyright © 1978 by Ray and Catriona Smith
All rights reserved
LCCN 78-66614
ISBN 0-689-30672-5
Printed in Great Britain
by W. S. Cowell Ltd.
Bound by A. Horowitz & Son / Book Binders
Fairfield, New Jersey
First American Printing, 1978

"Whoops!" cried Barley and fell off the cliff.

"Quick, Jacko," said Teddy. "To the rescue!"

Barley plunged towards the sea where two girls were practising water ballet.

"Excuse me. Have you seen Barley?" asked Teddy.

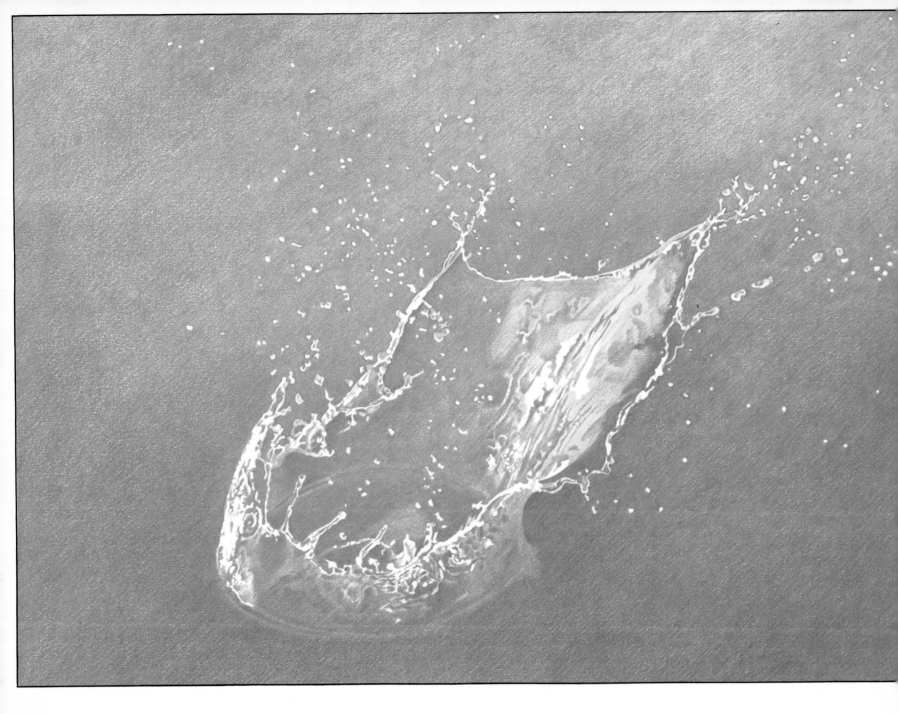

Splash!

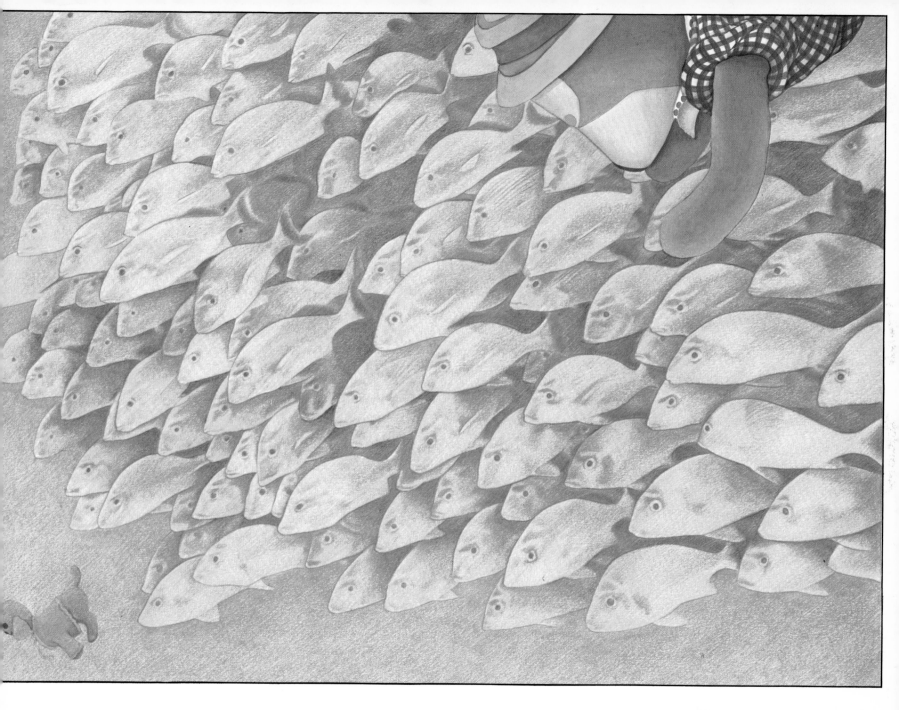

"I can't see Barley anywhere," said Teddy.

"Help!" shouted Barley. "A crab!"

Jacko forced the crab's claw open. "You're safe now, Barley," said Teddy.

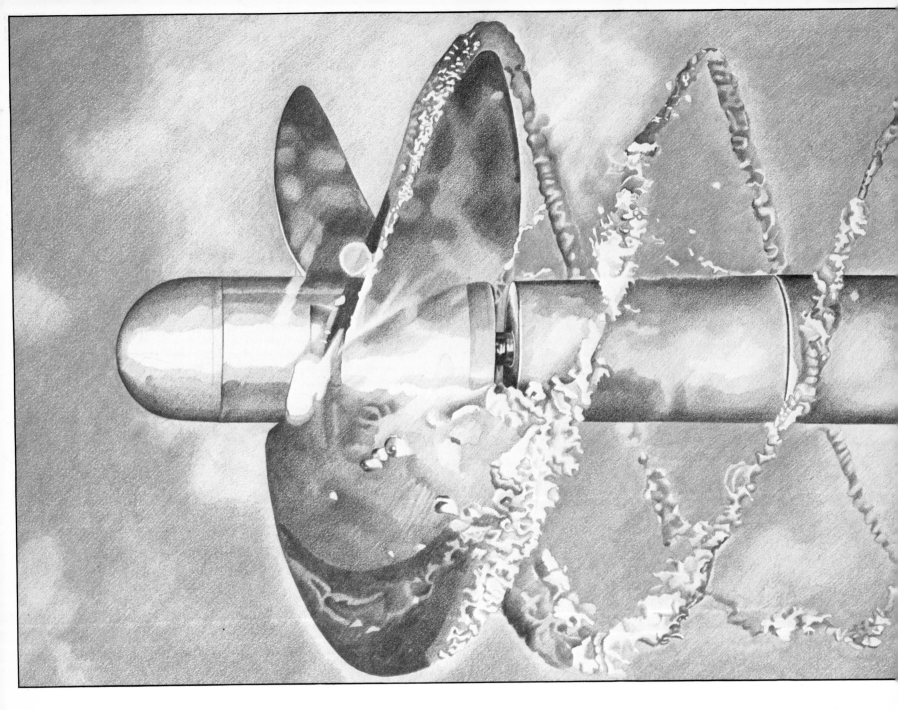

"Maybe he'll give us a lift," said Jacko.

. . . but the submarine swept on.

They tumbled down the continental shelf.

"Oh, a monster!" gasped Barley. "Nonsense," said Jacko, "just a large octopus."

"I'm off," thought the octopus and squirted ink at the animals.

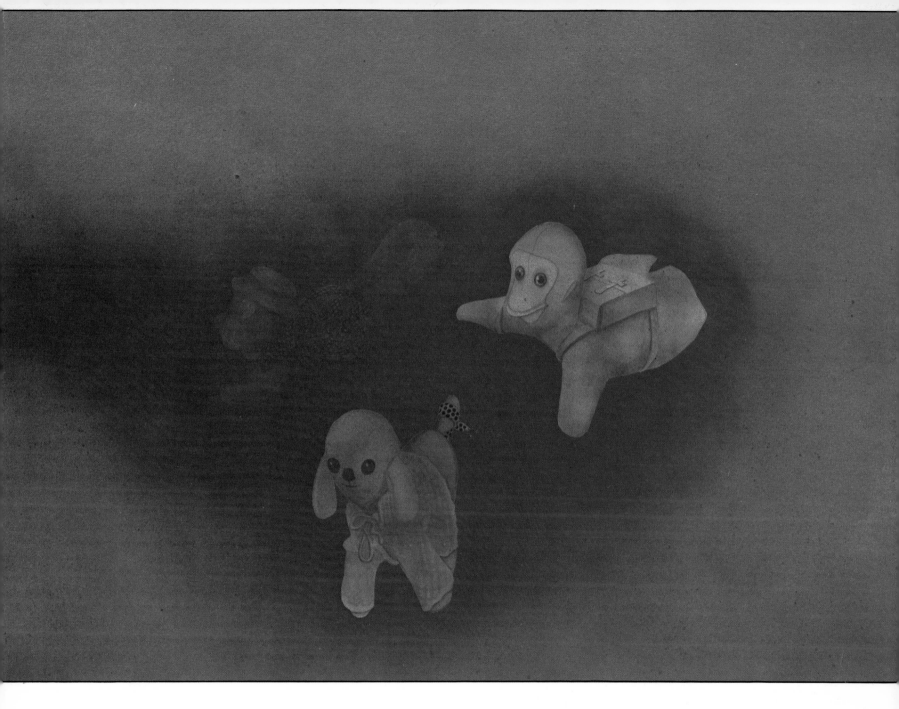

"Filthy stuff!" muttered Jacko.

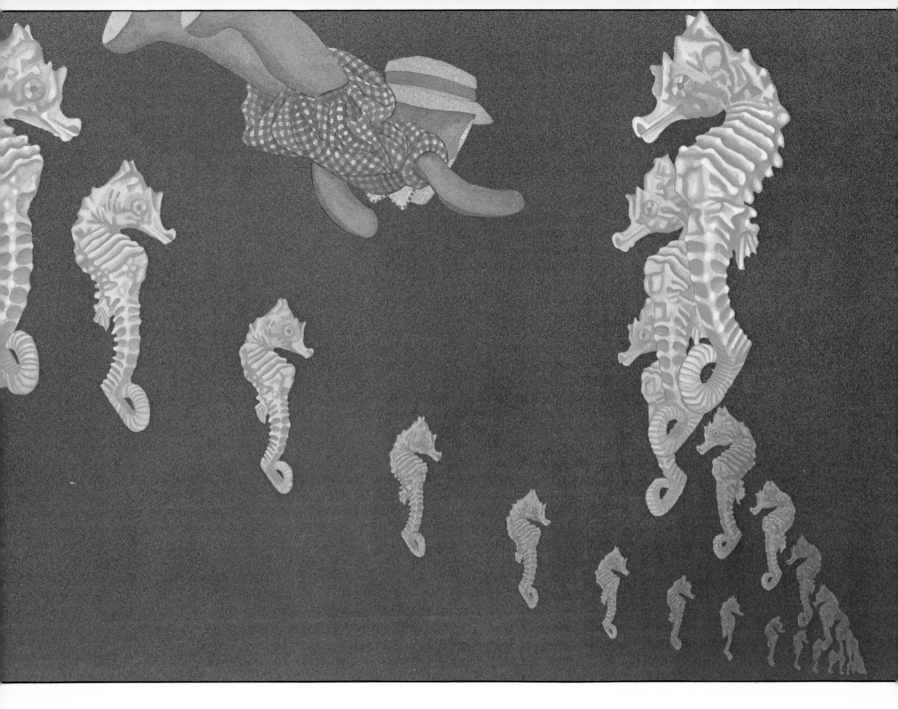

"This way," said Teddy.

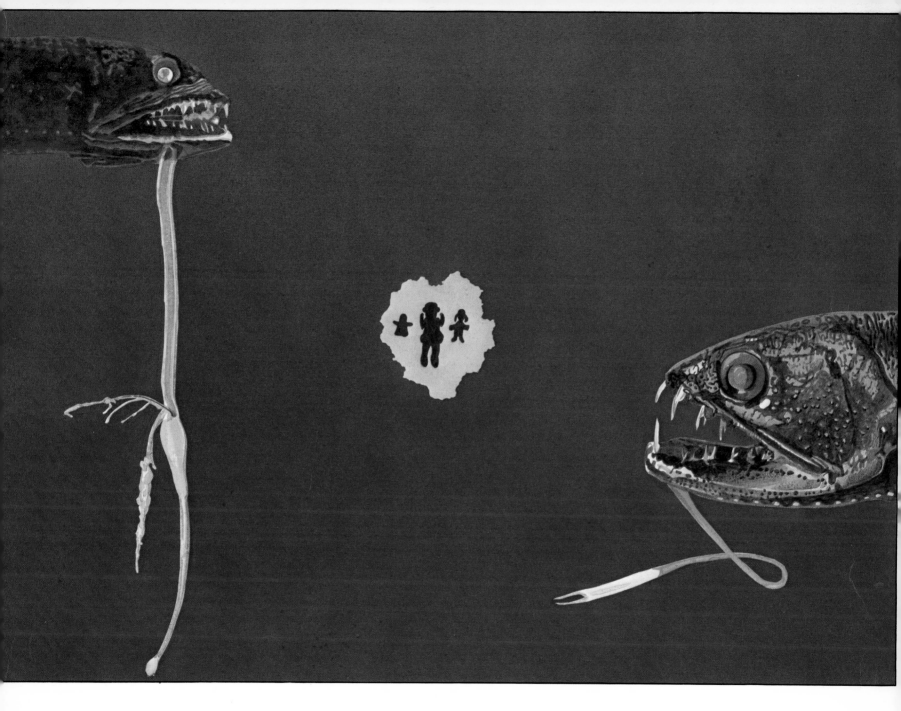

They swam to the mouth of a cave past strange luminous fish in the depths of the ocean.

"Look at those mermaids," whispered Barley. "Magnificent!" exclaimed Teddy.

"Smashing," said Jacko.

The mermaids' cave faded away. "I could have watched them for ever," thought Barley.

"How about some fish fingers?" said Jacko.

"Time to go," said Teddy and they shot up towards the surface.

"Ah, fresh air," said Barley.

They lay on the beach in the sun. "This is the life," murmured Jacko.

R